The Magical Wishing Fish

The Classic Grimm's Tale of the Fisherman and His Wife

Loek Koopmans

Floris
Books

Once upon a time a fisherman lived by the shore of a wide sea.

One day, he caught a fish and was reeling in his line when he heard a small voice calling, "Stop! Please let me go! I'm not a fish, but an enchanted prince. Put me back in the water and let me swim free!"

The fisherman was amazed. He'd never met a talking fish before.

"Of course I'll let you go!" said the fisherman, who was called Thomas. He carefully placed the fish back in the water and, quick as a flash, it swam away, disappearing beneath the waves.

When Thomas arrived home,
he told his wife Isabel about
the talking fish.

"An enchanted prince!"
she cried. "Did you wish
for anything before you
set it free?"

"No," said Thomas.
"What would I wish for?"

"I'm sick of living in
this broken old pot!"
Isabel sighed. "I wish
we lived in a little cottage
instead. Please go back
and ask the fish to make
my wish come true."

Thomas didn't want to ask the fish for anything, but he did want to make his wife happy, so he went to the high cliffs and called out across the calm water:

"Oh fish, little fish in the blue-grey sea,
Will you please come back to me?
My wife would like you to grant a wish.
Are you a magical wishing fish?"

The fish swam up to the surface. "Well, what does she want?" it asked.

"My wife is sick of living in a broken old pot. She would prefer a little cottage," Thomas told the fish nervously.

"Go back to your wife," said the magical fish. "Your wish has been granted."

When Thomas arrived home, he found
Isabel sitting outside a little cottage with
a small garden and a family of hens.

"Are you happy now?" he asked.

"I'm quite happy," she said.

But before long, Isabel had decided
the cottage was too small. "I wish we lived
in a tall castle," she said. "Please go back
and ask the fish to make my wish come true."

Thomas didn't want to ask the fish for anything,
but he did want to make his wife happy, so he
went down to the shore and called out across
the rippled water:

> "Oh fish, little fish in the blue-grey sea,
> Will you please come back to me?
> My wife would like you to grant a wish.
> Are you a magical wishing fish?"

The fish swam up to the surface.
"Well, what does she want?" it asked.
   "My wife thinks our cottage is too small.
She would prefer to live in a tall castle,"
Thomas told the fish shyly.
   "Go back to your wife," said the
magical fish. "Your wish has been granted."

When Thomas arrived home, he found
Isabel standing on the steps of an enormous
stone castle. It was so tall it reached high
into the sky.

"Are you happy now?" he asked.

"I'm quite happy," she said.

But after a few days, Isabel had another
wish. "I would enjoy living in our castle
even more if I were a queen," she said.
"Please go back and ask the fish to make
my wish come true."

Thomas didn't want to ask the fish for anything,
but he did want to make his wife happy, so he
went down to the shore and called out across
the rough waves:

> "Oh fish, little fish in the blue-grey sea,
> Will you please come back to me?
> My wife would like you to grant a wish.
> Are you a magical wishing fish?"

The fish swam up to the surface. "Well, what does she want?" it asked.

"My wife would like to be a queen," Thomas told the fish, sighing.

"Go back to your wife," said the magical fish. "Your wish has been granted."

When Thomas arrived home, he found Isabel wearing
a golden crown. Two servants were holding her beautiful
gown, which was covered in sparkling rubies.

"Isabel, now that you are a queen, are you happy?"
he asked.

"I'm quite happy," she said.

But after a few days Isabel told him, "I'm tired of just being a queen. I wish to be Emperor of all the land! Go back and tell the fish to make my wish come true."

Thomas didn't want to ask the fish for anything, but he did want to make his wife happy, so he went down to the shore and called out across the dark, crashing waves:

> "Oh fish, little fish in the blue-grey sea,
> Will you please come back to me?
> My wife would like you to grant a wish.
> Are you a magical wishing fish?"

The fish swam up to the surface.
"Well, what does she want?" it asked.
"My wife would like to be Emperor
of all the land," Thomas told the fish
reluctantly.
"Go back to your wife," said
the magical fish. "Your wish
has been granted."

When Thomas arrived home, he found Isabel
sitting upon a golden throne.

"Isabel," he said, "now that you are Emperor
of all the land, surely you must be happy?"

His wife looked down at him from up high.
"No, Thomas, Emperor is not enough! I want
to live like God! Go back and tell the fish to
make my wish come true."

Thomas didn't want to ask the fish for anything, but he did want to make his wife happy, so he went down to the shore and called out through the raging storm:

"Oh fish, little fish in the blue-grey sea,
Will you please come back to me?
My wife would like you to grant a wish.
Are you a magical wishing fish?"

The fish swam up on the crashing waves. "Well, what does she want?" it asked.

The fisherman fell to his hands and knees, ashamed. "Oh little fish!" he cried. "My wife has gone too far this time. She wishes to live like God!"

"Go back to your wife," said the magical fish. "Your wish has been granted."

When Thomas arrived home, he was amazed to find his wife waiting for him beside their old broken pot, smiling.

"Isabel," he asked, "can you be happy with a simple life once more?"

She took his hands and said, "Being rich and powerful did not make me happy. God on earth lived a simple life full of love and kindness, and I'm happy to live like that too." And they danced together in the warm sunshine.